The PEACOCK PARTY

(A SEQUEL TO)
THE BUTTERFLY BALL
and the
GRASSHOPPER'S FEAST

BY
ALAN ALDRIDGE

ILLUSTRATED IN COLLABORATION WITH
HARRY WILLOCK

VERSES WRITTEN WITH
GEORGE E. RYDER

A Studio Book

The Viking Press · New York

Also illustrated by Alan Aldridge

THE BUTTERFLY BALL AND THE GRASSHOPPER'S FEAST
with verses by William Plomer
THE SHIP'S CAT
with verses by Richard Adams

Illustrations and text Copyright © Aurelia Enterprises Ltd 1979
Published in 1979 by The Viking Press
625 Madison Avenue, New York, N.Y. 10022
Library of Congress catalog card number: 78-68811
ISBN 0-670-54549-X

Based on *The Peacock 'At Home'* by A Lady (1807), a sequel to
The Butterfly Ball and the Grasshopper's Feast

Printed in Italy by A. Mondadori Editore, Verona

Dragonflies and gnats, all bugs that creep or crawl,
Chorused in praise of the Butterfly Ball.
Mice and weevils, toads and rats,
Jigged to its theme and tossed up their hats.
It was hummed by the Beetle, then buzzed by the Fly,
And fiddled by crickets with a chirruping cry.
It was carolled by centipedes, squeaked by the Mouse,
Strummed by the Snail in his wallpapered house.
It was kneesed-up by newts, and crooned by the Vole,
Mumbled by Mole in his deep-chambered hole.
Wooed to by Frog, can-canned by Spider,
Wailed by the insects that wriggled inside her.
Ants, moths and ladybirds all heard the call,
And sang in loud praise of the Butterfly Ball.
Stoats, hornets and wasps all attended with pleasure,
But birds not invited were wroth beyond measure.

Sir Perceval Peacock, the famous millionaire
(The aristocrat, the dandy, the apogee of flair),
Displayed his bright plumes in a dazzling fan
And, addressing his fluttering colleagues, began:
"Friends, Romans and countrybeaks…"
(He used such quotations on every occasion,
Thinking they lent him a sage-like persuasion!)
"Shall we, like domestic inelegant males,
As boring as weevils, as sleepy as snails,
Sit humdrum at home and listen to spouses,
While mice, crickets, butterflies open their houses
To chirp, dance and sing with such vigour and gall
That terrible theme from the Butterfly Ball?
If these insolent airs are allowed to prevail
May Juno forthwith pluck the eyes from my tail!
A Party's proposed — at grand Perceval Mansion
(Late Renaissance, Art Deco, Baroque Imitation,
Rococo, Gold Grapes, Picture Palace collation!)
It must be before the Annual Migration!"

The missives went by Pigeon Post
A thousand leagues — from coast to coast.
The Woodcock preferred his lone haunt on the moor,
And Traveller Swallow was still on his tour.
The Cuckoo, who should have been one of the guests,
Was rambling on visits to other birds' nests.
But the rest all accepted the kind invitation,
And much bustle was caused in the feathered creation,
Such grooming of plumage, such preening of coats,
Such chirping, such whistling, such clearing of throats.
Such polishing bills, such oiling of pinions
Had never been known in the feathered dominions.

LOVE IS ALL
(FROM THE BUTTERFLY BALL)

THE TAILOR BIRD

The Tailor Bird offered to make up new clothes
For all the young fledglings who wished to be beaux.

I am the Tailor Bird, a most happy soul,
To please everybody is my only goal.
I cut, I press and sew all day,
And sing this little roundelay:

The Silkworm brought some silk today;
I paid him a penny and sent him away.
The Widow Spider brought fine silver thread;
I stitched her a trousseau for when she gets wed.
With a tra-la-la and a tra-la-lee,
There isn't a happier bird than me!

Behind me are hung my most famous creations:
Clothes that are triumphs in ten different nations.
It's the cut of my costumes that makes them unique —
My suits are bespoken by every smart beak.
That jaunty white wig for the Black Gull's sleek head
I embroidered myself with a gossamer thread.
Miss Parrot's pink gown is the best Kashmir silk,
And studded with pearls that glisten like milk.
The bodice is cut from fine Nottingham lace,
With five hundred stitches to hold it in place.
That fine russet waistcoat for poor Robin's breast
Fitted so neatly around his stout chest.
Alas, he encountered a most tragic end —
I lost a good client as well as a friend.
Of all my feathered friends the fowl
I most dislike is grumpy Owl:
As well as short-sighted, he's mean and rough —
And none too wise: he's usually stuffed.
Sometimes I work by candlelight
Into the stilly, starlit night.
I hear Miss Nightingale's dulcet note,
Bubbling forth from her silvery throat.
I know very well that I won't grow rich,
As I press, then measure, cut, then stitch.
But I'm still better off than most of you,
Doing what I was born to do!"

THE EAGLE

The magic day at last was dawning;
Chanticleer announced the morning:
"Today's the day, be up and away!
Peacockadoodledoo! Peacockadoodleday!"
Swifts and rooks and every guest,
In fancy plumes, their Sunday best,
Swept towards the Peacock Party,
Led by the Eagle, stern and haughty.

When the world at the time of Genesis stood,
Fashioned first by fire, and then by flood,
When earth and sea had separated,
And all the mountains elevated,
The Eagle was made ruler of the sky,
The arbitrator over all that fly.
Since might is right is inflexible law,
He was chosen by battle of beak and claw.
When the conquering Roman horde
Put the world beneath their sword,
Were not the mighty legions led
By the Eagle at their head?
Did not the old Germanic race
The Eagle effigy embrace?

OSWALD OSTRICH, R.A.

Cranes came from Egypt and larks from Brazil;
The Ostrich loped down from his house on the hill.

Oswald Ostrich, R.A.
Has, on any given day:
Bats in the Belfry
Lions in the Den
Locusts in the Oven
Gravy on his Pen
Gold coins in woolly socks
Turtles in the Pool
Cheetahs in the Card-Room
Whales in the Hall
Lilies in the Tea Pot
Banknotes in the Shed
Honey on the Chandelier
Snakes asleep in bed
Beggars in the Bathroom
Watches baked in batter
Monkeys in the Studio
— As mad as a hatter.

THE DODO'S DREAM

The Dodo had too many ports for the road,
And dropped off to sleep in his cosy abode.

The clock crowed twice at ten to three
(He hadn't wound it up, you see).
The Dodo cried: "Lop off his head!"
Baby Dodo's in his bed.
To breakfast now on Stilton cheese,
With feather soup and legs of fleas.
But first I'll have a Dodo doze,
A dream-filled, delicate repose:
I'll spin far away to the rest of my race,
Through endless time and limitless space.
I'll wing over sea and I'll wing over sand
And spend a few hours in my Dodo land.

The grass is blue and sweet to eat,
Strewn with fruit and nuts and meat.
All the nests are made of silk,
The rivers run with white goats' milk.
The Dodos fill the earth and sky,
The Gryphon grins as he flaps by.

THE RAVEN

The Raven, however, was far from delighted;
He cursed at the party; he wasn't invited.

Before the world found shape or rhyme,
Before the pendulum measured time,
You were spawned by a murky spell,
You bedmate of demons and powers of hell!
Haunter of the gallows tree,
Raven, what mysteries do you see?
What hellish schemes do you devise?
What evil brews in your cruel, coal eyes?
Busy in your time-worn tower,
You spin your black charms hour by hour:

"Take sulphur's fumous air,
  Mercury, potassium mix with care,
  Charge this broth to gentle fire,
  Add bat fur, cobweb — stir this mire.
  Then your evil wish behold:
  The ruddy hues of magic gold!"

THE STORY OF THE MIGHTY PARROT, SHEL-EM-NAZAM

An awesome guest soon joined the throng
Though, fortunately, not for long.
The bustling birds looked up in wonder,
Seeing Shel-em-Nazam and his infamous Condor
From a golden throne threatening cruel demands,
More jewels and more wealth from his conquered lands.
His eyes gleamed darkly and then he was gone,
Casting a shadow across the sun.

Many stories have been told
Of tyrants, despots, villains bold.
Worst was the parrot, Shel-em-Nazam,
Spawned by a she-devil, sired by a ram.

Birds reviled and cursed his name,
As he warred with sword and flame.
His palaces gleamed on a misty hill;
They say he changed his form at will.

He sacrificed to the Evil One
In the pagan Temple of Golden Sun.
And demonstrated his evil powers —
Issuing edicts from silvery towers.

Though evil passes as evil must,
And palace and parrot both turn to dust,
A thousand years later tales may be told
About carvings in stone and slivers of gold
That are found by the banks of the old Amazon
Bearing the claw mark of Shel-em-Nazam.

For no one can ever be sure, my friends,
Where truth begins and fiction ends.

MADAME BELLA DONNA

The Shrike swept in from Zanzibar;
King Crow croaked down from a cool kulibar.
The Toucan took to a smooth Rolls Royce,
But Madame Swan made a more curious choice.

Madame Bella Swanna,
Such a prima donna,
Came upon a
Carriage, the finest ever seen:

Opal, diamond, sapphire,
Crystal, emerald, ruby,
Turquoise and topaz and aquamarine.

Madame Bella Donna,
Such a lovely swanna,
Set the beaks a-clicking,
Set all hearts awhirl.

With her lazurite and moonstone,
Amethyst and zircon,
Jet, jade and filigree
And deep sea pearl.

L'OISEAU ORCHESTRA

Let the party commence! To the garden repair,
Full of jasmine and tulips and daffodils, where
An orchestra is preparing to play
Throughout the night till the dawn of day.

L'OISEAU ORCHESTRA

Serenade your hearts delight — Throughout this very special night

Sir Tom Titt — Maestro

Wilbur Woodpecker — Pizzicato

Petronius Puffin — Obbligato

Penelope Parrot — Adagio

Paulus Pigeon — Pianissimo

Claude Cockatoo — Larghetto

Tobias Thrush — Allegretto

Benjamin Blackbird — Trillando

Orville Owl — Andantino

Septimus Sparrow — Rallentando

Neptune Nightingale — Profundo

Carmine Canary — Soprano

Frederick Finch — Amoroso

Each and every one a brilliant virtuoso!

Canto Canto mia Passa

FOR YOUR OBVIOUS ENJOYMENT
AND BENEFIT

THE INCOMPARABLE

The World's Weirdly Wonderful Wizard

METAMORPHEUS

MASTER MAGICIAN AND *ILLUSIONIST*

ENTERTAINS

with his numerous and bewildering

EFFECTS

HOCUS POCUS

THE *KING* of *KARDS*

SURPRISING AND STARTLING TRICKS

made possible by sleight of hand and manual dexterity

LEVITATION

(£20 to anyone able to discover levers, wires or any other
underhand means of manipulating the floating turtle)

ASTROLOGICAL FORTUNE TELLING

THE ART OF LEGERDEMAIN

The confounding Conjuration of the

DECAPITATION FEAT

A living bird's head suspended on a common tea tray –
10 feet above its body, whistles, chirps, sings and

SMOKES HAVANA CIGARS

THE
GRAND FINALE

BEING

THE AMAZING, EXTRAORDINARY

FLOATING ZODIALOGICAL
CRYSTAL BALL

An incandescent display of PYRO ASTROLOGICAL
NECROMANTIC SIGNS

AS SEEN BY HER MAJESTY

THE QUEEN

LADIES AND GENTLEBEAKS, I DRAW THE ATTENTION OF ALL THOSE
DESIROUS TO LEARN MAGICK TRICKS ETC. ETC., THESE CAN BE
TAUGHT IN A VERY SHORT TIME

CHARGES ON APPLICATION

METAMORPHEUS

THE AMOROUS ADVENTURES
OF COLONEL RUDDY-FOWL STORK,
OF STORK HALL, STORKSHIRE.

The wooing strains of the tango
Mixed with the scented air.
This was the prelude to Perceval's Party
And all the élite were there.
And Colonel Ruddy-Fowl Stork
Was pining for Purity Crane:
He'd long tried to win and to woo her —
But alas, so far in vain.
He made his way to the terrace,
To preen and imbibe the air.
He glanced around once in the shadows —
And saw Purity Crane was there.

And while the other guests were mingling,
The terrace couple felt a tingling . . .
They talked of groves and of migrating;
They spoke of nesting and of mating.
They danced into the afterglow
And saw the moonlight come and go.
They did what birds in love should do,
With first a bill and then a coo,
Dancing sweetly cheek to cheek,
Kissing warmly beak to beak.

And in deep velvet of the night
He lay beside his heart's delight.
But with the early morning light
Sweet Purity had taken flight.

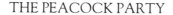

Resplendent in the marble hall which glowed with fretted gold,
The princely Peacock sat in state, the party to behold.
Lace, and Flanders cambrics, shot silks of every hue,
Swirl with scarlet tunics, confectioned gold and blue.
There were lions, frogs and hippos — a marvellous parade —
Then jokers, jesters, harlequins joined in the masquerade.
All came with tributes laden: with pearls from Mandalay,
With gold, with diamonds, emeralds, and ivories from Cathay.
Lord Pelican gave a ruby, the fiery "Burmese Star",
Count Cockatoo brought sandalwood, Kingfisher caviar.

But descriptions must fail, the pen is unable
To describe the delights which covered the table.
Every delicate viand that taste could detect:
Wasps *à la sauce piquante*, and French flies in *vinaigrette*.
Worms and frogs *en friture* for all web-footed fowl,
Stuffed shrew, spiced mice and spiders to tempt the grumpy Owl.
Nuts, grain, fruit and fish regaled every beak;
The overfed Pelican can't even speak.
Penguins serve groundsel on fine silver dishes,
Fountains spray champagne to quaff as one wishes.

They filled all their crops with the dainties before them,
Then cleaned off their bills, and, with utmost decorum,
Went to the ballroom where the loud trumpets' blare
And the strains of soft melodies soon filled the air.
First the Peacock and Toucan danced a gavotte,
Then Ostrich performed his bizarre Turkey Trot.
Close by, the Thrush and Blackbird vied,
To sing "Bird Songs at Eventide".
Miss Jenny Wren, soprano, trilled, full of love,
Her world-famous solo "Oh for the wings of a dove".

Then Chanticleer, scenting a new day was dawning,
Gave out his clarion call as a warning.
So they chirped in full chorus a friendly adieu;
With hearts light as plumage, away they all flew.
Then long live the Peacock in splendour unmatched,
Whose Ball shall be talked of by birds yet unhatched.